CU00403971

Where Silence Prays

Jared Cade is the number one bestselling author of *Agatha Christie and the Eleven Missing Days*. He is a former tour guide for a bespoke luxury travel company, escorting parties around Agatha Christie's home, Greenway, which is now owned by the National Trust. During an appearance on the British television quiz *The $64,000 Question*, he won the top prize on his specialist subject of Agatha Christie's novels. Jared Cade is also the creator of the Lyle Revel and Hermione Bradbury mysteries. His work has been published in over a dozen languages. For more information about the author, please go to www.jaredcade.co.uk.

Also by Jared Cade

Agatha Christie and the Eleven Missing Days

Murder on London Underground

Murder in Pelham Wood

Jared Cade

Where Silence Prays

SCARAB BOOKS

Published by Scarab Books
2022 © Jared Cade Limited
Jared Cade has asserted his right to be identified as
the author of this work under the Copyright,
Designs and Patents Act 1988.

ISBN: 9798357179685

Cover Design by GermanCreative

Dedicated to Sizza Watts,
descendant of Sir Isaac Watts (1674–1748)

CONTENTS

Requiem for the Dead

The squabbles of our wondrous life,
Unfurl in bitter pain and strife.
Guilt burning deep within,
Begs forgiveness of our mortal sin.
After a life of blood, sweat and toil,
So ends our moment on this blessed coil.
As the wreath-laden casket departs,
Memories comfort anguished hearts.
And the promise of eternal days,
Fills the void where silence prays.

Jared Cade

'Without the shedding of blood
there is no forgiveness of sin...'

Hebrews 9:22

Where Silence Prays

Father Lambourne heard about the prison breakout from his sister. Edith was waiting for him at the front door of the presbytery. She was looking like a disapproving dragon whose demeanour belied her deep affection for him. Light spilled from the narrow hallway behind her into the deserted street of drab terraced houses that were covered with decades of black grime from the long-defunct collieries. The accusatory look on her elderly face told Father Lambourne that he was late getting home. The aroma of cooked food wafted down the hall from the dining room and he was conscious of feeling light-headed because he had not eaten all day.

'Three men broke out of Wimslow Prison

earlier today,' she said grimly.

Father Lambourne spoke in a soft, fluting voice that was unexpectedly beautiful in tone despite his advanced years. 'Oh, no, why didn't anyone tell me?'

'It was announced on the radio after you left this morning,' said Edith. 'Everyone probably assumed you knew. The police have arrested two of the men within the last hour.'

'Thank goodness for small mercies.'

'One of them is a rapist,' continued Edith. 'The other is an armed robber − a former war hero, would you believe?' She added with a shiver of dread, 'The third prisoner is still on the run.'

'Wimslow Prison is twenty-five miles away,' said Father Lambourne reassuringly. 'I can't see him making it this far.'

Edith shut the front door against the cold December weather and made a gesture to help him off with his overcoat.

'No, I haven't got time,' said Father Lambourne wearily. He longed to go upstairs, change his shirt and put on a warm jumper, but he knew he wouldn't be able to tackle the stairs until the pain in his arthritic knee subsided. 'I'm expected in church in twenty minutes.'

'It's going to be even harder to capture this man now night has fallen,' said Edith, tut-tutting to herself.

Father Lambourne did not envy the police their difficult task. 'The escaped prisoner is probably feeling cold and frightened,' he said, 'and more of a danger to himself than others.'

'He's a convicted child killer,' said Edith, pressing her lips together in a thin line of disapproval.

'I'll make sure I lock up properly before we go to bed,' said her brother with a worried frown. 'There's no point taking unnecessary risks.'

With his mane of white hair and pale complexion, Father Lambourne was a well-known figure amongst churchgoers in the riverside town of Grimstoke in North Yorkshire. He had spent most of the day visiting parishioners who were unable to attend regular services at St. Cuthbert's owing to their poor health or octogenarian fragilities. His meeting with the new local councillor hadn't gone well. Everyone was stretched for money these days and Father Lambourne was reconciled to finding another way to raise the necessary funds for the repair of the church roof.

Over the years the members of Father Lambourne's congregation had dwindled as the old died off and the young moved south in search of jobs. The ruins of the castle and the railway viaduct crossing the River Nidd afforded summer visitors, who came for half a day at the most, the only real scenic attractions Grimstoke had to offer. Father Lambourne knew he ought to have retired years ago, but his more stalwart parishioners relied on him so much for spiritual guidance and support especially during the bleak winter months. The windows of the shops in the nearby town of Market Leeming were brightly lit with jolly effigies of Santa Clauses, grinning elves and frolicking reindeers. Christmas trees glittered with beautiful lights, exquisite baubles and tinsel, as well as divine angels, topped off with a fairy-tale dusting of snowflakes, all promoting the good will and happiness of the yuletide season. The reality for many residents of Grimstoke is that Christmas was a time of bare necessities for those already living close to the bone and their only solace lay in their Christian faith.

Over dinner in the dining room, Edith returned to her former grievance. 'It's such a cold night everyone is bound to remain inside with their doors locked. You shouldn't be going anywhere while there's an escaped prisoner on the run.'

Inwardly Father Lambourne agreed, but he felt obliged to say, 'If I don't hold confessional I might forfeit the opportunity to save a soul in torment.'

He was quick to express his appreciation of the meal Edith had cooked. Asparagus soup was followed by a lukewarm kipper, mashed potatoes and fresh peas. The three bars of the electric fire were not adequate enough to heat the dining room, and he was grateful the heavy green curtains were drawn over the windows to exclude any hazardous draughts. Two of the wall sconces cast a convivial glow over the mahogany dining table while the third needed its bulb replacing. The low murmur of the wind against the windows left him feeling curiously cocooned from the outside elements. He was obliged to forego cheese and coffee.

'All this gadding about at your age isn't good for you,' said Edith pointedly. 'We'll have to hope the police find the missing prisoner sooner than later.'

'It shouldn't take them long to locate him,' said Father Lambourne soothingly. 'The police helicopter is equipped with thermal imaging equipment. Tom Everett is an excellent pilot.'

'A man like Tom should be at home with his

wife and two young children on a night like this,' grumbled Edith. 'You're better off staying indoors and keeping warm. If you're not careful you'll catch cold. Remember what happened to our mother. Dead of double pneumonia within a fortnight.'

'The good Lord will take me when he sees fit.'

'That's no excuse for not wearing a muffler,' added Edith anxiously. 'If you want my opinion there's little chance of anyone coming to confessional tonight.'

Father Lambourne found two dejected-looking individuals, huddled in coats and scarves, waiting for him on his arrival at St. Cuthbert's. After listening to their sins and granting each of them penance, he slumped back in his seat and listened to the last penitent's footsteps receding into the distance. Silence closed around him. Owing to the bitterly cold weather he doubted if anyone else would come to confess their sins. He would wait three-quarters of an hour before locking the church up for the night. Inside the confessional booth, a wave of inertia came over him and his eyelids grew heavy…

Presently Father Lambourne released a gentle sigh that sounded like air escaping from a pair of bellows. Caught in the shadowy no man's land between sleep and memories, he tried to return to the warmth of his slumbers, but the tide of his recollections was too strong. An unidentified sound somewhere near at hand reminded him inexplicably of ten-year-old Tommy Sparks. The grimy-faced urchin was always getting up to mischief. He was accompanied everywhere he went by a devoted bull terrier that never seemed to mind if the child treated him roughly or pulled his tail. A fragment of verse by Dr Isaac Watts, the 17th century theologian, dropped unexpectedly into Father Lambourne's mind:

'Let dogs delight to bark and bite,
For God has made them so:
Let bears and lions growl and fight,
For 'tis their nature, too;

But, children, you should never let
Your angry passions rise;
Your little hands were never made
To tear each other's eyes —'

The rest of the verse eluded Father Lambourne. His watery blue eyes opened slowly and a cold shudder passed through him. He had been remembering his early days as a curate. Tommy Sparks' name was engraved on the stone war memorial in the centre of Grimstoke. He had died for his country in his twenty-third year.

Father Lambourne had been away at the time serving another parish. A prolonged period of treatment for polio had prevented him from being conscripted and many had assumed he would not make old bones. That must have been at least four or five decades ago now. These days Father Lambourne's thoughts were returning to the past with a frequency that unsettled him. The aftermath of his dream left him feeling disorientated and it took him two or three minutes to adjust fully to his surroundings. The wait for someone else to enter the confessional booth on the other side of the grille and ask for penance had proved long and futile.

Silence pervaded the small church. There was no heating. It was far too expensive to put on. The circulation in Father Lambourne's left leg was made worse by cramp. For additional warmth he was wearing his overcoat beneath his cassock. The smell of rotting plaster and mildew from the leaking roof, along with incense and candlewax, tainted the air and was as familiar to him as the rhythm of his own heart.

He found himself wondering what Tommy Sparks might have done with his life. The phrase 'he gave his life for his country' covered a multitude of horrors and was of no more comfort to the bereaved than the meaningless phrase 'he died a hero.' Tommy Sparks had never aspired to be a hero although his posthumous VC had immortalised him as one in the minds of everyone in Grimstoke. His parents had been inconsolable with grief when their only son was laid to rest in the churchyard.

Father Lambourne shivered as Sir Thomas Browne's words came to him from centuries ago: '*Life is a pure flame and we live by an invisible sun within us.*' He was conscious of a weakening of his pulse, of a fading light somewhere deep within him. His life force was ebbing slowly away. He dreaded to think what would happen to his beloved St. Cuthbert's after his lifetime. Although not normally superstitious, he had the extraordinary belief – no, *conviction* – that he was going to die tonight.

'*This night thy soul shall be required of thee.*' The parable of the rich man was hardly applicable to

Father Lambourne. He had precious little in the way of material possessions to bequeath to anyone. Poor Edith would struggle to make ends meet after his lifetime. The shock of losing her husband all those years ago had turned his sister sour and since then she had grown to rely on him as much as he depended on her.

Stifling a yawn, Father Lambourne glanced at his watch. It was just after ten o'clock. He must have fallen asleep two or three hours ago. The shock jerked him fully awake and he felt a dull thud in his left temple. He felt old and tired and worn out. It was time he took himself off home. Edith would have retired for the night by now. Before he went to bed he would stoke the kitchen Aga and –

The sound of low intermittent sobs reached him through the grille. The discovery that he was not alone produced a flurry of heart palpitations within his emaciated frame. His visitor must have entered the church while he was sleeping.

'You sound as if you're in a great deal of pain,' he said with compassion. 'I'd like to help.'

The sobbing broke off abruptly and the ensuing silence was punctuated by a woman replying in a distraught voice, 'Everyone has forsaken me – or they will when they find out what I've done…'

Father Lambourne suspected she was in her twenties or early thirties – well-educated – not one of his regular parishioners. A stranger, in fact.

'It isn't true, you know,' he said in his most persuasive voice. 'God is on your side. Even when you feel as if the people you love have forsaken you and the whole world has turned against you. All you have to do is reach out and ask Him for help.'

She sounded confused and frightened. 'I wish it was as simple as that.'

'It's essential for someone entering into confession to have the intention of returning to God like the prodigal son and to acknowledge their sins with true sorrow. Have you examined your conscience before coming here tonight and told God of your remorse?'

The woman sounded startled – unsure of herself. 'Yes – yes, I have…'

Father Lambourne waited for her to utter the time-honoured words. 'Bless me, Father, for I have sinned…'

'When did you last confess your sins to God?'

'It was at least four years ago – possibly longer.' The woman's resolve wavered then steadied itself. 'During that time my marriage has gone from bad to worse.'

'You need to go back in your mind,' said Father Lambourne, 'to a time when your relationship with your husband was happy and focus on that.'

She was silent for a few moments and then, as her resistance crumbled, she spoke in a tear-bloated voice, 'It all seems so long ago. I don't see how dredging the past up is going to help me now…'

'Tell me about your relationship with your husband.'

Father Lambourne's innate gentleness and humanity proved as soothing as a balm. Like numerous penitents before her, the woman drew a deep breath and began unburdening herself to him.

'My husband and I were childhood sweethearts. Each day I went to school he would ride alongside the bus on his bicycle. I'd lean out of the window and we'd swap love letters… It was his ambition to become a soldier and see the world. I was frightened I might never see him again, but he kept his promise after he joined the army and married me… The early years of our marriage were relatively carefree. The Afghanistan War has since blighted so many lives. Following his return, he became a lot moodier and depressed. Recently he's taken to drinking and shouting at me. There have been times when I felt I was married to a stranger…'

'You've got to find a way to help your husband to forget the past,' urged Father Lambourne, 'and concentrate on the future.'

'That's really no longer possible…'

'We all have regrets,' said Father Lambourne sympathetically. 'It's only natural in times of great stress to say "what if" but if we must say "what if" we should refrain from saying it about the past and instead say it about the future.'

'My husband once said the horrors he witnessed as a soldier would always be with him. That's why I encouraged him to leave the army and to become a successful businessman.'

'You did the right thing by urging your husband to put the past behind him.'

The swiftness of her response made it clear he had struck the wrong note. It was apparent that more than the cold was making her voice tremble.

'Lately I – I've felt so frightened of him. It's a horrible feeling when the man you love most in the world wishes you were dead. Tonight something in me snapped *and I killed him…*'

The blood drained slowly from Father Lambourne's face. For several seconds he wondered if he had misheard her, but he knew he hadn't. A lifetime's experience of conversing with his parishioners convinced him that she was telling the truth. His voice was charged with horror and outrage.

'*You killed your husband?*'

'Yes…'

'*Murder is a mortal sin.*'

'In my case there are extenuating circumstances,' replied the woman in a jerky voice.

Father Lambourne's heart fluttered against his rib cage like a stricken dove denied flight. An instinct for self-preservation urged him to have nothing further to do with her.

'There are no extenuating circumstances when it comes to murder,' he said. 'Have you forgotten the meaning of the Ten Commandments? If you've got any conscience at all, *I want you to repeat them now…*'

On the other side of the grille the stranger was silent. There was no way of knowing what she planned to say or do next.

'Repeat after me: *"I am the Lord thy God. Thou*

shalt have no other gods or graven images and likenesses.'"

Silence.

"'Thou shalt not take the Lord's name in vain,'" he continued. *"'Thou shalt remember the Sabbath day – thou shalt honour thy mother and father – Thou shalt not kill…'"*

Was it his imagination or was that a stifled sob?

'You've broken your wedding vows,' he said, struggling to speak in a calm voice. 'You've surrendered yourself to evil…'

'I tried to be a good wife for my husband's sake,' she said. 'But it wasn't easy being married to a former soldier. The index finger on his right hand was blown off by a landmine. The past came back to haunt him every time he looked at his hand. His mood swings were so unpredictable. I never meant to –'

Father Lambourne's heart palpitations frightened him. The blood was pummelling in his ears.

'There can be no excuse for murder,' he said hoarsely.

In the tense silence that followed he hoped she would leave. She had brought hatred and dissent into his beloved St. Cuthbert's. A feeling of light-headedness came over him. He was hypoglycaemic and the sugar levels in his blood had dropped. It was too late now to wish he had eaten some cheese after dinner in accordance with his usual ritual. He felt desperately in need of hot coffee to banish the chill inside his body and soothe his troubled soul, but such a wish – even if it could have been granted just then – would only have led to a disturbed sleep owing to his worn out bladder. The presbytery's Victorian lavatory gurgled like an angry beast roused out of its slumber and was apt to wake Edith up in the room next door after which she always found it difficult to get back to sleep.

The silence in the church was so absolute that Father Lambourne wondered if the woman had left without telling him. He almost choked on his next utterance.

'Tell me why you killed your husband...?'

The woman's voice welled up with emotion and her reply made him flinch. 'I – I couldn't cope with his cruelty any longer. It – it had got so bad I considered taking my own life...'

'You had only to reach out and this church would have helped you,' said Father Lambourne sternly.

'My husband was a very difficult man. You've

no idea what he put me through...'

Father Lambourne spoke in measured tones. 'The true path to a Christian life lies in *forgiveness...* It's so much easier to forgive others when we realize a simple basic truth of life – we're all sinners... A lack of forgiveness results in bitterness – and bitterness brings bondage in the form of anger, sorrow and conflict... The desire to address a wrong – whether real or imagined – the urge to take revenge upon someone or something that has offended us – only serves to remind us that bitterness is an eternal cul-de-sac... Before God can save us, *it is imperative we humble ourselves by forgiving others so He in turn can forgive us...*'

'You probably think I'm full of hatred,' she said. 'But I still love Adam *and I always will...*' Her voice cracked and she was unable to go on.

Father Lambourne had difficulty capturing his breath. *'You don't know the meaning of the word love or you could never have killed your husband.'*

'That's not true,' she protested.

'The seal of the confessional is inviolate,' he said. 'No one will ever know why you came here tonight or what we spoke about. Having heard your confession I'm unable to offer you penance.'

He leaned forward to catch a glimpse of the

woman's face on the other side of the grille. The sudden movement set off a twinge of pain in his arthritic knee. Her features were obscured by shadows although he could hear her whimpering.

'Have you forgotten about the two thieves on the cross?' she asked tremulously. 'One repented his sins and went to Heaven.'

Father Lambourne drew his breath in sharply. 'I also know about the other thief who descended into Hell.'

'We're all sinners,' she repeated, stifling a sob. 'And it's never too late to repent. Isn't that what the Bible teaches us?'

'Your husband was an honourable man who fought for his country,' said Father Lambourne, wondering if his words would prick her conscience. 'You are the person he trusted most in this world.'

'Adam saw too much carnage while he was in Afghanistan,' she said. 'Drinking was the only way of blotting out the terrible memories he carried around with him. Despite his success in business, he was never satisfied and took his anger and frustrations out at the shooting range. Lately his anger and drinking had spiralled out of control. I would never have shot him tonight if he had shown me the respect I deserve.'

'You had no right to act as your husband's judge, jury and executioner,' said Father Lambourne coldly.

'That's easy for you to say,' she said with a flash of scorn in her voice. 'Adam Butler fooled most people into thinking he was Mr. Perfect. But he was far from the pillar of the community everyone believes. I'll never forget the disgust I felt when I found out he was having an affair with a sleazy waitress. The suffering he's put me through is unbelievable.'

'That's still no excuse,' said Father Lambourne. 'Your actions are totally immoral – an abomination against Christ.'

The woman's voice sharpened. 'When I agreed to become Adam Butler's wife adultery was not listed in our marriage vows. This afternoon we had another argument. He refused to give his mistress up. I threatened to tell the police about the illegal Beretta he brought back from Afghanistan. Adam told me that if I betrayed him he would slash my face so no man would ever look at me again. I was so angry I drove over to Market Leeming and did some shopping on his credit card. On the way home, I stopped off for a couple of drinks.'

Father Lambourne winced. 'You were wrong to turn your back on your problems.'

The woman was in the grip of such a powerful emotion that she didn't appear to hear him. 'It was already dark by the time I reached home. The air in the living room was thick with cigar smoke. The smell of it almost made me retch. Adam just sat there with his back to me watching TV. I told him that if he left me for Jacqueline *I was going to kill him.*'

Father Lambourne felt compelled to listen to her against his will. Outside the wind butted the church and shook the trees in the graveyard. An icy-cold draught eddied up the chancel. It violated the confessional booth and clawed its way up his legs and made the muscles in his chest contract painfully. He was conscious of his breath leaving his mouth in a visible vapour.

'I can't believe I'm hearing this,' he said hoarsely.

'Adam refused to apologise for all the pain he'd put me through,' she said on a rising note of hysteria. 'I told him if he had one shred of decency left in him he'd give Jacqueline up. It was obvious his precious game of football was more important to him than our marriage. The arrogant bastard just ignored me. He'd done that to me so often in the past. You can't imagine how *angry* that made me feel.'

'You're going to have to live with the guilt of your actions for the rest of your life,' said Father Lambourne.

'Adam had drunk far too much as usual. He'd knocked over an ashtray and hadn't bothered to pick it up. The mess had fallen all over his scarf and the empty beer bottles lying on the floor. And I knew – I just *knew* – I was expected to clean the mess up. I was so disgusted with him. Something in me snapped –'

A shudder passed through Father Lambourne and he momentarily closed his eyes. 'What did you do next…?'

'There was a pistol on the sideboard. Adam must have been planning to clean it before he was summoned to the phone. I picked it up and shot him in the back of the head before I knew what I was doing…'

The elderly priest was unable to stifle the moan that came to his lips. 'Your actions are beyond despicable,' he said. '*They're utterly indefensible…*'

The woman was lost in an agony of torment. 'It happened so quickly. He slid out of the armchair and slumped facedown on the hearth rug.

One of his wrists was pinned beneath him. I tried feeling the other wrist for a pulse and couldn't find it...'

'Evil has entered your heart,' said Father Lambourne with a tremor in his voice, 'and now there's no turning back...'

'At first I was so distraught I thought I was going to throw up or pass out. Somehow I managed to hold myself together. After drinking some scotch, I – I couldn't bring myself to stay in the house any longer. I've been driving around ever since – wondering what to do with my life...'

Silence pervaded the church.

Father Lambourne rubbed his hands together in a bid to restore the circulation in them. Snow was forecast in the days ahead. If the pundits were right Grimstoke was set to have its first white Christmas in over a decade. It rankled him that there were other people in the parish who were far more deserving of his compassion and help than this wretched woman. At this time of the year a lot of elderly and vulnerable people had a choice of either buying food or heating their homes; they couldn't afford to do both. It was a cause of great sorrow to him that he couldn't do more to help them.

'I'm unable to grant you absolution,' he said. 'Your actions are truly reprehensible. I must ask you to –'

'There's something I'd like you to do for me first,' she interrupted him, as if reading his thoughts, 'and then I'll leave…'

On the other side of the grille, Sheila Butler opened her handbag and stared at the Ruger .22 semi-automatic pistol with which she had shot her husband. Her cheeks were wet with tears.

'I've got no reason to go on living now that Adam is dead,' she said. 'But I want God to know I've forgiven Adam for hurting me... I want God to grant Adam entry into Heaven… Would you mind saying a prayer to help his soul on its way…?'

Father Lambourne was taken aback by her unexpected request. Perhaps he had misjudged her. It was possible she really had loved her husband after all.

'Are you saying you've forgiven your husband for having an affair?' he asked in a puzzled voice.

'Y-yes, yes, of course I have,' she said defensively. 'What does it matter? I've got no right to expect forgiveness, but that doesn't entitle you to speak to me as if I'm a second class citizen.'

'That was certainly not my intention,' said Father Lambourne, humbled by her outburst. 'If I am to point out the error of your ways and lead you back to God, I must know why you let evil enter your heart.'

Sheila Butler's gaze wavered and her voice dropped almost to a whisper. 'The line between love and hate became blurred. I pulled the trigger without giving any thought to the consequences of my actions...'

"'*Guilt burning deep within begs forgiveness of our mortal sin…*'" quoted Father Lambourne.

'What do you mean by that?' she asked.

'People should make love instead of war. Mankind is constantly threatened by disease, famine and death, as well as innumerable slings and arrows attributed to outrageous fortune… Love is our only defence against these perils – the love we feel for our fellow human beings and the love we share with our Lord Jesus Christ…'

'My grandmother's love for my grandfather didn't keep him safe during the Second World War,' she said bitterly. 'One day she told me, "You'll never hear a soldier saying he hates the enemy, but the women do because they don't have to do the shooting. *Women hate more than men…*'"

Father Lambourne had never hated anyone in his life and yet he suspected there was considerable truth in what she was saying.

'That didn't give you the right to shoot your husband,' he said sharply.

'Life isn't as black and white as you think,' she continued scornfully. 'I've been driving around for hours thinking about my actions. I'm going to have to live with them for the rest of my life and there's nothing I can do about it... We live in a world of double standards. Society quite rightly condemns an armed robber who leaves a trail of bloodshed in his wake. Yet when the police shoot a terrorist dead while he's on a killing spree no one really minds or cares – possibly apart from the dead man's family... Even when the police kill an innocent man in mistake for a terrorist and public outrage follows, his death is cited as a "regrettable necessity." No one is held accountable...'

Father Lambourne recognized she was trying to gain his sympathy. He was far too wise an old bird to fall for such an obvious ploy. A toxic brew of anger and sexual jealousy had prompted her to shoot her husband. She was now wrapping herself up in a protective bubble of self-deception and attempting to justify her actions in order to deceive him into thinking she was the victim of her marital problems rather than her murdered husband.

'Terrorism is a form of war,' he said authoritatively. 'The police have a duty to protect society. National security has always taken precedence over the rights of individuals dedicated to terrorism in the same way a man suffering from leprosy is isolated in a colony to protect the healthy from falling victim to the disease. Terrorists have turned their back on God and worship false idols. Such individuals are like derelict ships that drift in the darkness and wreck the sound, seaworthy craft. But their behaviour in no way excuses private individuals like you who have flouted the rules of society and killed on a sudden neurotic whim.'

'I'm not saying it does,' she said petulantly. 'But you can't deny life has a way of being messy and full of inconsistencies. Adam once said war is about older men making decisions that send younger men to their deaths. After a soldier returns home and gets a medal pinned to his chest, he's forced to live with the knowledge he's a killer and not the war hero everyone thinks. He's obliged to bottle his feelings up inside *because if he confides in his wife she'll wish he hadn't.* If he opens up to her without being asked she'll claim she still loves him as much as she always did. But it isn't true, you know, because it nearly always changes the dynamic of their relationship. Some wives leave their husbands *because they can't accept they're married to a man who has killed repeatedly to survive*... So the truth is invariably swept under the carpet so both parties can get on with their rose-tinted, petit bourgeois lives...'

Father Lambourne's upper denture shifted and rubbed against his mouth ulcer. 'You've strayed from the path of righteousness,' he said in a tone of genuine sorrow. 'What others have done before you in no way lessens the enormity of your sin or excuses your actions…'

'Do you seriously think I don't know that?' she said impassionedly. 'I'm the first to admit women can be just as ruthless as men. We say we're not, but we know we're lying and we do it on purpose to get our own way. Doctors and nurses help women have abortions every day of the week and no one bats an eyelid. Afterwards they blame the man for getting them pregnant rather than their own sexual desires for leading them into temptation.'

'Comparing yourself to others will only increase your bitterness,' said Father Lambourne firmly. 'Two wrongs don't make a right...'

'I've confessed to my sins,' she said helplessly.

'What more do you want?'

'Confessing to your sins is not the same as repenting,' said Father Lambourne. 'Repentance produces *change* whereas remorse merely produces *sorrow*. The man who has a change of mind and actively turns away from sin is repentant while the man who wallows in tears and wishful thinking without turning away from sin is simply remorseful. You could have spared your husband's life tonight, but you chose not to. It had nothing to do with the line between love and hate becoming blurred. If you couldn't have your husband *no one else was going to....*'

His remark struck a raw nerve and Sheila Butler's defiance crumbled.

'All I know for certain now,' she said, 'is that I've crossed the line between good and evil – and the line has widened into a huge black abyss. There's no turning back for me – no making amends for what I did... Knowing others have sinned helps me to understand myself and cope that little bit better...'

'If only you had come to me first,' said Father Lambourne.

'It wouldn't have made any difference,' she said, struggling to regain her self-control.

'Jacqueline saw her chance and deliberately came between Adam and me. She wanted him because she couldn't find anyone else. You probably won't believe me, but I'm truly sorry I shot Adam. A red mist came down over my eyes and before I knew what I was doing –' Her voice trailed off and she had difficulty going on. 'Nothing you can say will ever come close to competing with my own self-recriminations. I – I came here tonight because I need you to say a prayer for Adam. Is that asking too much…?'

Father Lambourne's expression softened visibly. 'I'll join you in saying a prayer for your husband,' he said slowly, 'on one condition…'

Sheila Butler's voice tightened. 'What is it?'

Father Lambourne was careful to speak in a calm, unhurried voice. 'If you're genuinely determined to repent, then first it is only right you should report your husband's murder to the police.'

The harshness of her response indicated he had underestimated her.

'Y–you're asking too much…'

'There's a police station just across the road,' said Father Lambourne in his most persuasive tone.

He was aware the recent cuts in the police budget had led to staff shortages. The officers who manned the police station had probably been called to Muswell Police Headquarters to help with the search for the escaped prisoner. Still, there was just a chance the police station might be staffed.

'The police are highly experienced,' he said. 'They'll be sure to understand. If you like, I can come with you –'

Animosity flared in her voice. *'No, I'll do no such thing…'*

Father Lambourne was left in no doubt that he had chosen the wrong words. An unexpected wave of fatigue swept over him. It left him feeling drained of energy. Sudden bouts of breathlessness were one of the penalties of being old and only having one lung. The other had been removed years ago to prevent the cancer from spreading. If only this wretched woman would stop contaminating his beloved St. Cuthbert's with her self-pitying diatribe and leave him in peace. The door of the confessional booth always opened noiselessly. The sound of the woman's high heels rapping on the flagstones outside told him she was leaving. Without giving conscious thought to his actions, his eyes shot open and he looked out of the confessional.

'Where are you going?' he asked.

'It's really none of your business,' she replied defensively.

'And yet you made it my business by coming here tonight,' he said. 'The true path to redemption lies in repentance. It's imperative you go to the police and confess your sins. Someone might find the body and be falsely accused of killing your husband.'

Startled, she swung her tear-stained face round to look at him. She was a willowy brunette, elegantly dressed, surprisingly attractive and far younger than he had imagined. Her green eyes were hard with defiance and some other emotion – fear? Or was it anger?

'You mean like his mistress Jacqueline?' A smile curled the corners of Sheila Butler's lips and then she laughed. 'Oh, I'd like *that* to happen – *I'd like that a lot.*'

She fell silent, turning the matter over in her mind, then she drew the Ruger out of her handbag.

'All I have to do is go to Jacqueline's house before she gets home from work,' she said. 'I'll hide the murder weapon among her belongings. *When the police find it they'll think she killed him...*'

Father Lambourne realized he had

underestimated Adam Butler's wife. There was a dangerous glint in her eyes. She was far more intelligent and conniving than he had imagined. It was possible she might succeed in framing her rival. If Jacqueline were clever enough she might convince the police that Adam Butler had been murdered by his wife. Or there again – the police might never find out who had killed him...

Father Lambourne suddenly wondered if the woman standing before him was right to suspect her husband of having an affair? There were plenty of jealous wives in existence who suspected the worst of their husbands without any tangible proof; they were frequently so fearful of being abandoned that they couldn't reconcile themselves to being married to a loyal and loving man. Was the murdered man's wife like that? Or had he really committed adultery? Would someone in his mistress' position, with her living to earn as a waitress, have entered willingly into an affair with a man like Adam Butler? A man with supposedly deep emotional problems, alcoholic tendencies, and a morbid fascination for guns?

'What's the matter, Father?' Sheila Butler smiled vindictively at him. 'Does the thought of Jacqueline taking the blame for my actions bother you?'

Father Lambourne groaned out loud. 'Is that what you want to happen?' he asked.

'Jacqueline is a home-wrecking slut! She deliberately set out to steal Adam from me. You can't stop me from framing her for his murder. Everything I say within the confessional is confidential.'

'You have no right coming here and making me an accessory after the fact to your heinous crime.'

'One of the advantages of going to confessional,' she mocked, 'is that it entitles a person to sin all over again with a free conscience.'

Sheila Butler suddenly laughed. It crossed Father Lambourne's mind that she was far more volatile than he had originally perceived – possibly even unhinged...

'*I want you to leave*,' he said, struggling to catch his breath.

'Oh, I'm not going to hang around any longer.' She glanced at the small gold Cartier watch on her wrist and smiled again. 'Jacqueline's shift at the restaurant in Market Leeming will be over in another couple of hours. Thanks to your guidance, Father, *I've got other fish to fry*.'

Father Lambourne spoke in a voice tinged with

defeat. 'I'm not in a position to tell anyone what you've said…'

She smiled gloatingly. 'That's right – you'll burn in Hell if you do.'

'You'll only feed your hatred for Jacqueline if you take her freedom away from her.'

Anger lanced Sheila Butler's voice. *'That bitch is going to pay for stealing my husband.'*

Father Lambourne's plan to urge her to confess to her husband's murder had backfired. Her desire for self-preservation was matched by an equal desire for revenge.

'Do you seriously want to destroy another person's life?' he said incredulously. 'Think of your own soul before you answer my question.'

Sheila Butler's eyes flashed. *'Yes, I want to destroy Jacqueline Rawlinson in return for all the pain she's caused me…* Adam would never have looked outside our marriage if it hadn't been for her… She's totally shameless and deserves to pay for what she's done to me…'

Father Lambourne took an involuntary step forward. A nail, protruding from the side of the confessional booth, caught on his cassock and overcoat, jerking them both open. Underneath he was wearing a white shirt. *It bore the bloodstained imprint of the murdered man's right hand.*

The look of gloating anticipation on Sheila Butler's face turned to shock and disbelief. 'W–why are you covered in *blood*?'

There was no way Father Lambourne could deny the bloodstained handprint on his shirt belonged to Adam Butler because the right index finger was missing. Until tonight he had never met the murdered man's wife. He cursed his bad luck. He ought to have remembered about the nail. He had snagged his cassock on it in the past.

'I went to your house earlier this evening,' he said.

The bewildered expression on her face indicated she was not sure if she had heard him correctly.

A squirt of saliva passed Father Lambourne's bloodless lips. An extraordinary coincidence had brought Sheila Butler here to confess to a murder he himself had committed. He wondered if it had occurred to her that one murder so often leads to another. He had to keep her talking while he decided what to do next.

'*My shirt is covered in your husband's blood.*'

She appeared lost for words.

'That was my scarf lying on the living room

floor,' added Father Lambourne. 'It must have fallen off during the struggle.'

She stared at him uncomprehendingly. *'What struggle?'*

'Your husband wasn't watching television when you returned home,' he said.

'How can you be so sure –?'

'He was already dead.'

Sheila Butler blanched. 'W–what are you saying?'

Father Lambourne's voice thickened with emotion. '*I killed him…*'

He saw fear glitter in his visitor's eyes and then he clenched his jaw as memory reclaimed him.

Adam Butler was a tall, imposing man with wavy black hair, cruel, sensual lips and a strong jaw that hinted at a steely determination to get his own way in everything he did. He was sitting in the living room of his Edwardian house on the outskirts of Grimstoke watching a football match on TV when the front doorbell rang. He rose swiftly with his customary air of masculine assurance, ushered his guest into the living room and sat back down in the leather armchair he had vacated.

'You're two hours late for our meeting, Father Lambourne.'

Adam Butler's voice was as smooth as malt whiskey and it was easy to understand why women found him so attractive.

'I'm terribly sorry,' said Father Lambourne, feeling unaccountably flustered. 'I'm sure the mistake was entirely mine. My memory isn't as good –'

'My wife Sheila is out,' said Adam Butler. 'I expect she's gone shopping. What I'm about to say to you is in total confidence – at least for the time being.' His last utterance had a faintly ominous ring to it.

'I'm grateful to you for seeing me at this late hour,' replied Father Lambourne politely.

Cigar smoke hung heavily in the air and the only source of light came from the TV screen and a nearby table lamp. He stifled the urge to cough for fear of offending his host and blinked as his eyes adjusted to the gloom.

Adam Butler took a long drag on his cigar before stubbing it out in an ashtray. A Beretta 9mm semi-automatic pistol was lying on the coffee table waiting to be cleaned. He picked it up and began polishing it with a white cloth.

'The reason I asked you here this afternoon is because money is missing from the church restoration fund.'

Father Lambourne's heart missed a beat. 'You must be mistaken –'

'You've been helping yourself to it,' said Adam Butler, speaking with a razor-sharp edge to his voice that made it clear he did not tolerate fools gladly. 'The council asked me to audit the books. You've been giving the money to the poorer members of the parish.'

Father Lambourne's heart missed a beat. *'No, you're mistaken –'*

'In the short time I've lived in Grimstoke I've been doing some checking up on you. If the council were to give you any more money for the repairs of the roof you'd only give it away.'

Father Lambourne continued to deny the accusation. But Adam Butler was not deceived. In addition to working for the local council, he was a highly experienced accountant and successful businessman. He was angry about something and Father Lambourne wondered if he had argued with his wife Sheila before she left the house. The way in which Adam Butler was waving the Beretta about as he spoke was truly unnerving. It was apparent he had been drinking heavily.

'*You're a disgusting thief, Father Lambourne.* I'm going to make it my business to report you to the church authorities. Before that it's only right you should have the opportunity to return the money.'

Adam Butler helped himself to another bottle of beer and took a long pull on it. Several empty bottles littered the carpet around the armchair. He seemed too drunk to notice or care.

'I only gave to those in desperate need,' said Father Lambourne. 'They had no idea where the money came from. I can't return the money. It's simply not possible –'

Adam Butler's temper was dangerously close to snapping. 'If you renege on my ultimatum I'll make you sorry...'

'You're asking too much,' protested Father Lambourne feebly.

Adam Butler shot up out of his armchair, his eyes blazing with fury. '*You just pushed your luck too far!*'

Father Lambourne gave a startled cry as the other man loomed over him with the gun in his hand. The look of savage determination on Adam Butler's face frightened Father Lambourne. All at once, he found himself locked in a desperate struggle with his host for supremacy of the gun. His scarf fell to the floor and an ashtray containing cigar butts was overturned in the terrifying scuffle that ensued.

There was a loud shot –

Father Lambourne's eyes widened in shock and disbelief. The expression on Adam Butler's face was one of blank amazement. The gun fell to the floor and skittered out of sight beneath the coffee table. Adam Butler clutched his chest, then his bloodstained hand shot forward pushing his guest away from him. He staggered backwards, collapsing into the leather armchair in front of the TV.

Father Lambourne's heart was thudding wildly. The glazed look in Adam Butler's eyes filled him with a shudder of revulsion. If he hadn't known any better he might have thought Adam Butler was still watching the football match…

It was extraordinary how easy it was to murder someone. Father Lambourne had been hoping the Beretta would go off and kill Adam Butler while he was polishing it. When that hadn't happened he had deliberately tugged on Adam Butler's arm during their struggle…

By the time Father Lambourne reached home

he had pulled himself together. It had been his intention to go upstairs before dinner and change out of his bloodstained shirt, but the pain in his arthritic knee had prevented him from climbing the stairs to his bedroom. Edith's watchful presence had made it impossible for him to dispose of the shirt in the kitchen Aga.

Over dinner, she had rebuked him for going out without his muffler. What she hadn't known is that he had left his muffler behind at Adam Butler's house. In his abnormal state of mind, he supposed he had left the presbytery without it that morning. Edith had noticed nothing amiss during dinner although he had felt unusually hungry.

Sheila Butler was staring in shock and horror at Father Lambourne. The discovery that she had not killed her husband turned swiftly to outrage and anger.

'*I can't believe I trusted you!*' she hissed.

Father Lambourne felt a surge of fear. 'You ought to have taken my advice,' he said, '*and left here…*'

'*You're not going to get away with this,*' she said. '*I'm going to the police.*'

'Aren't you going to ask why I killed your husband?' said Father Lambourne, stalling for time. 'I went to him for help, but he accused me of stealing from the church restoration fund.'

Sheila Butler's eyes narrowed suspiciously. 'Adam was scrupulously honest. He must have discovered you're not.'

Father Lambourne shivered uncontrollably. 'As much as I denied having anything to do with the defalcations, he refused to believe me. He was polishing his Beretta. It went off during our struggle. He was shot in the chest – and died almost at once...'

Sheila Butler shook her head in bitter self-reproach. 'I had no idea Adam was already dead when I saw him sitting with his back to me in front of the TV...'

'It was an accident – I swear that's all it was...'

'You pulled the trigger on purpose,' she said coldly. 'Do you know what you are? You're a self-righteous hypocrite. I can't believe I could have been deceived by you. You've no right to call yourself a man of God.'

'You're right about one thing,' said Father Lambourne in a tremulous voice. 'We're all sinners. Under the circumstances we've both got too much to lose by telling anyone what happened.'

'I'm not going to let you get away with killing Adam!'

'I'm an elderly man and I'm dying.'

Sheila Butler pointed the Ruger at Father Lambourne. The expression in her eyes was hard and unwavering. Father Lambourne's bowels threatened to turn to water and he hoped he would be spared the terrible indignity of losing control of them. He was about to die. He knew he didn't deserve her compassion because he had not demonstrated any towards her husband. Over her shoulder, he saw the altar triptych depicting *Christ Triumphing Over Darkness and Evil* and he realized it was still possible to help her salvage the wreckage of her life.

'If you pull the trigger,' said Father Lambourne, 'you'll be crossing a line. The same one you crossed earlier tonight when you believed you had murdered your husband. God is giving you a second chance – this is a golden opportunity to cross back over that line before it widens into an abyss... The choice you make now will define the rest of your life. Don't throw it away in a fit of anger or pique. It's not what your husband would want...'

Sheila Butler's eyes glistened with tears and she held onto them with difficulty. 'How would you know what Adam wants?'

Father Lambourne next words reverberated with irony and he smiled at her in sorrow. 'It's still not too late for you to repent and bask in God's forgiveness and love…'

Sheila Butler held the Ruger steadily in her hand. 'How does it feel knowing you're about to die?' she asked.

A tremor of fear closed around Father Lambourne's heart like a cold hand. He understood then the desperation a gambler feels when all the chips are against him and his very existence hangs on the final roll of the dice.

'I've married enough couples during my lifetime to know when a woman is pregnant,' said Father Lambourne. 'Some might call it a gift or a sixth sense, but somehow I've always *known* –'

Sheila Butler's eyes narrowed and the tears at last rolled down her cheeks. 'Are you saying I'm pregnant?'

'Yes...'

'How do I know you're not lying?'

'I've run out of lies – and there's so little time left,' said Father Lambourne simply.

'You're right about that,' she said, smiling tautly at him as she prepared to pull the trigger. 'This bullet is for Adam and the child I was never able to give him –'

'Freeze, don't move!'

The order came from the police firearms officer who had just entered the church. He was pointing his Glock 17 at Sheila Butler. Within the last ten minutes the convicted child killer had been caught by one of the police units. On the other side of the road a team of firearms officers had returned to the temporary command post of the police station for a debriefing. It was unusual to see a light burning inside the church so late at night and the firearms officer had been sent to investigate.

Startled, Sheila Butler dropped the pistol. *'Officer, I'm Mrs. Adam Butler. This man has murdered my husband…'*

The bovine firearms officer recognized her and took one look at the priest's bloodstained shirt.

'Father Lambourne, is there any truth in the accusation?' he demanded in a deep, husky voice that resonated with authority. 'Why are you covered in blood?'

'My husband found out Father Lambourne has

been embezzling the church funds,' cried Sheila Butler. 'I came home from shopping and walked in on their argument. Adam's Beretta was on the coffee table waiting to be cleaned. Father Lambourne picked it up and threatened him with it. In a bid to save Adam's life, I grabbed the pistol lying on the sideboard. Father Lambourne shot Adam dead in the chest with the Beretta before I could stop him. As Adam stumbled and fell, I fired the pistol. He got in the way of the bullet intended for Father Lambourne...'

Father Lambourne looked into Sheila Butler's eyes and saw a glimmer of triumph in them because the seal of the confessional was absolute.

The firearms officer turned to the murdered man's wife and said, 'Mrs. Butler, you were seen returning home tonight fifteen minutes *after* Father Lambourne left your house.'

Panic seared her voice. '*Who told you that?*'

'You couldn't possibly have seen Father Lambourne shoot your husband,' said the firearms officer as the BWV camera attached to his uniform silently recorded their encounter.

'I've told you the truth,' she snarled.

'A woman who shoots her dead husband in the back of the head is guilty of attempted murder in the eyes of the law.'

Sheila Butler was rendered speechless with shock. Her plan to absolve herself of any wrongdoing in her husband's murder had backfired. A look of thwarted fury contorted her face.

The firearms officer's voice was hard and unrelenting. 'I must ask you both to accompany me to the police station for further questioning –'

A shudder shook Father Lambourne's body. He glanced around him wondering what would become of his beloved St. Cuthbert's. It had been wrong of him to embezzle the money, but so many of his parishioners needed handouts to survive from day to day. His gaze settled on the stained-glass window above the altar. The window depicted the image of Jesus on the cross. It looked so beautiful when the sun shone through it during the day. Now the unrelenting blackness of the night emulated the darkness in Father Lambourne's tormented heart and soul. Overwhelmed by the enormity of his sins, he felt utterly helpless – completely terrified and alone…

His heart palpitations had worsened. He was convinced he was dying…

'This night thy soul shall be required of thee…'

Having surrendered himself to evil, Father Lambourne recognized there was no turning back. His world was crashing down around him and there was nothing he could do to prevent it. There was only one certainty for him now...

Above him in the sky, the metallic roar of the police helicopter became deafening as it thundered over the boundary wall of the churchyard. It had been scrambled in the search for the escaped child killer. The thermal imaging equipment on board had enabled the pilot Tom Everett to locate the fugitive hiding in a ditch on the outskirts of Grimstoke before police officers on the ground had moved in and arrested him. The child killer was now being escorted under armed guard back to Wimslow Prison. Tom Everett was returning the helicopter to Sherbourne base before going home to his adoring family. As the helicopter passed above the east portal of the church he switched on the spotlight to get his bearings in the dark. The downdraught from the rotor blades was tremendous. One of the branches from an old oak tree broke off –

Everything seemed to happen after that in slow motion. The branch smashed through the stained-glass window of the church and sent debris flying in every direction. For a blinding instant, the pieces of stained-glass shone like jewels that swam and dissolved in the beam of the helicopter's spotlight before the occupants of the church were showered in falling shards of coloured glass, plaster and masonry.

The pain in Father Lambourne's chest was like a burning poker. He was convinced the Heavens had opened and the wrath of God was being unleashed upon him – and then he was embraced forever by a darkness greater than the night.

THE END

Let Dogs Delight to Bark and Bite

Let dogs delight to bark and bite,
For God has made them so:
Let bears and lions growl and fight,
For 'tis their nature to;

But, children, you should never let
Your angry passions rise;
Your little hands were never made
To tear each other's eyes.

Let love through all your actions run
And all your words be mild;
Live like the blessed Virgin's Son,
That sweet and lovely child.

His soul was gentle as a lamb;
And as his stature grew,
He grew in favour both with man,
And, God, his father too.

Now, Lord of all, he reigns above;
And from his heavenly throne,
He sees what children dwell in love,
And marks them for his own.

Isaac Watts

Printed in Great Britain
by Amazon